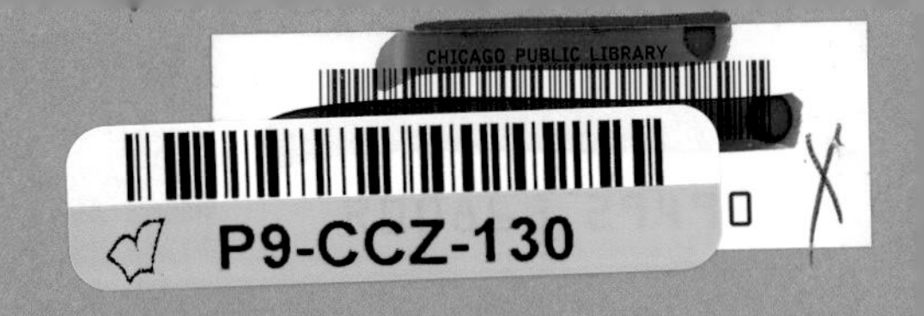
CHICAGO PUBLIC LIBRARY
P9-CCZ-130

THE BEAR ON THE MOON

JOANNE RYDER

ILLUSTRATED BY

CAROL LACEY

MORROW JUNIOR BOOKS

NEW YORK

To all children who wonder about things
and who look for the great white bear
when the moon is full
J.R.

At the top of the world, a winter night lasts a long time. It is then the storytellers share their tales of how the world began.

The small ringed seals say the great sea was made from the salty tears of the very first seals that were hunted long ago.

The snowy owls say the great snowstorms began when wolves chased the first white owl. To escape, he shed his feathers, blinding the wolves with their brightness.

But the great white bears tell a different story, and this is what they say....

When everything was new, there was nothing at the top of the world but the sea where the white bears lived. They hunted seals in the sea. They floated and played in the sea. They were bears of the sea, and the sea was their home.

But there was one bear who was different. She could hunt better, dive longer, and swim faster than any other bear. But she also wondered about things no other bear thought about. And sometimes she hunted for the answers.

"How deep is the sea?" she asked her friends.

"Deep enough," they said, but they did not really know.

So the curious bear swam down and down, farther than she could have imagined. She swam through dark waters with strange fish and squid, but even she could not reach the bottom of the wide, deep sea. Very tired, she swam up and up to find her friends.

"The sea is deep and very dark," she told them. "But the fish glow. There are so many tiny lights glowing and flashing in the dark."

"That's nice," said the bears, but they didn't really care.

Even so, the curious bear kept on wondering and asking questions.

Floating on the deep waters, she would look far across the great sea. And she'd wonder, *What is it like at the edge of the sea where the dark sky begins?*

Or she'd turn her furry head up and wonder about the round moon shining over her. "The moon shines like a big silver fish. Do you think bears live there?" she'd ask the old, tired bears who floated nearby.

But they had no answers for her.

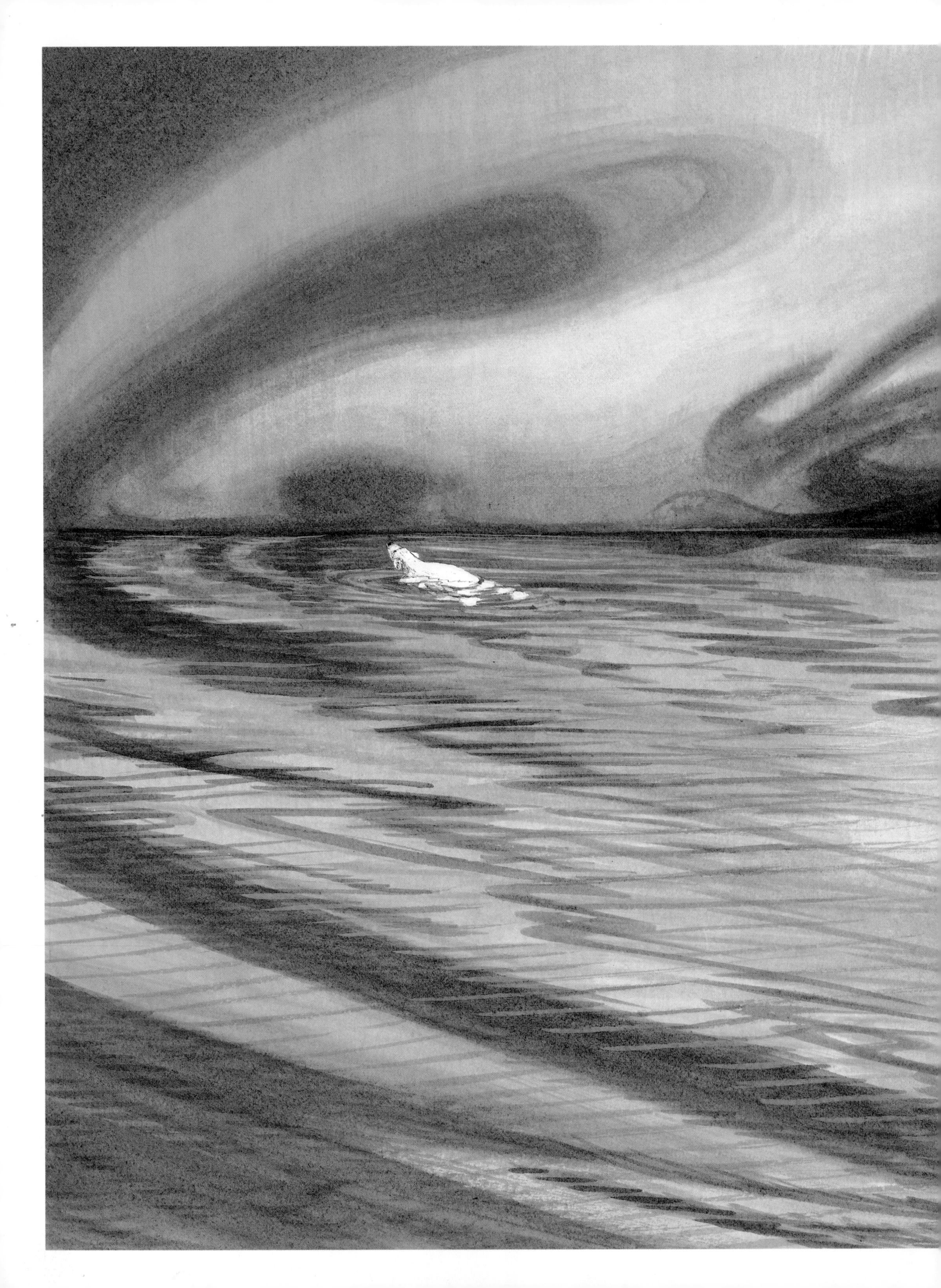

One night, the white bears say, the curious bear looked up at the sky and saw something new. Rising from the edge of the sea, lovely streamers of lights stretched high above her—moving, curling, softly glowing red and white and green.

"Look!" she called. "Look at the sky!"

"Ahhh!" sighed the bears, happy just to watch the twisting lights.

Only the curious bear wondered, *What could they be?*

She began to swim away from the other bears. The shimmering lights swayed across the sky, like seaweed moving in rough waters. And she thought, *If I can swim just a bit farther...*

Again and again, she coaxed herself to keep on swimming. At last, she swam to the place where the sea touched the sky and where the wonderful lights began. They reached up into the dark sky like a slowly moving staircase, stretching higher and higher to some place far above her.

Where do they go? she wondered.

The bear raised her front paws out of the water. The lights danced around her, changing her white paws to red and green. With all her might, she leapt from the sea into the air and landed on the stair of lights. All around her there was space, empty and dry, as she began to climb. When she looked down, she saw white bears floating, small and very far away.

As the bear climbed, the round moon drew closer. Finally, she reached the top of the stair of lights.

Could she really touch the moon?

Her paw stretched high till she touched something cold like the deepest waters of the sea, hard and slippery like the scales of a huge, shiny fish.

The bear climbed up onto the moon and walked for the first time.

All around her, the white bears say, she saw a rocky land covered with snow and ice. It was a bright, empty place, shining below a dark sky. A cold place, with no sea, and no white bears anywhere.

So this is what the moon is like, she thought.

And for the first time, the curious bear began to run. Her powerful legs stretched as she leapt over ragged chunks of ice. It felt good to run, and she wished the other bears could run with her.

She ran and ran until she was too tired to move. Then she curled up in a drift of snow and fell asleep. In her dreams, she saw bears running and resting and swimming in a world of sea and ice and land.

When she awoke, she looked down, way down, off the edge of the moon, and saw the bears far below. And she remembered her dream.

I will take some moon home, she thought. *Then the others will see how good this place is.*

She began to dig some of the ice and the rock beneath. She broke off big pieces with her paws, but they were too heavy for her to carry.

Perhaps I can throw them, she thought. So she tossed pieces of moon into the air with her powerful paws, until a big chunk flew high, then fell down and down...and floated in the deep, dark sea below.

Excited, the bear dug harder. *Splash! Splash!* More pieces of the icy, rocky moon fell into the sea.

The bear on the moon watched the white bears climb onto the cold ice. They slid and played, and the old, tired bears rested, happy to sleep so well at last. Mother bears made safe dens on the land where their little bears could rest, too.

And so the great white bears became ice bears, walking and running on the snowy land and the ice that covered patches of the great sea.

The bear on the moon kept tossing icy chunks into the sea, shaping the ice bears' new world. But one morning when she looked around her, the moon, which had shone so brightly before, was not there. Only a sliver of brightness was left, just where she stood.

Oh no, thought the bear. *It's all gone. I've given it all away.*

She walked across the sliver of moon to the stair of lights. As she leapt off the moon, the last bit of ice and snow fell to the earth. Behind her, there was only darkness.

Slowly, she climbed down the shimmering steps. Sadly, she walked on the ice-covered sea, and it reminded her of the moon that was no longer there.

The ice bears were happy to see her. "Look," they said. "Look at this wonderful thing that has happened."

"The moon's gone," she said. But they were too busy exploring new places to listen. Resting on the good ice, only the old bears stayed to hear. Half-asleep, they thought they dreamt the story she told them.

"I thought I could help us," she said. "But I didn't mean to make the moon disappear."

Though she felt sorry that the beautiful moon was gone, the curious bear saw wonderful changes in her world. Long-legged animals came to the land near the top of the world. Sea creatures–some with hard shells and some with many arms–clung to the rocks where the land met the sea. And new plants began to grow on the land that was once the moon. The bears and the animals grew strong and fat, eating the bright berries and sweet grasses.

The curious bear watched the new animals and learned their ways. And watching the world around her, she began to notice that there seemed to be a little less ice, even a little less land. The great sea slowly ate the land and melted the ice every day.

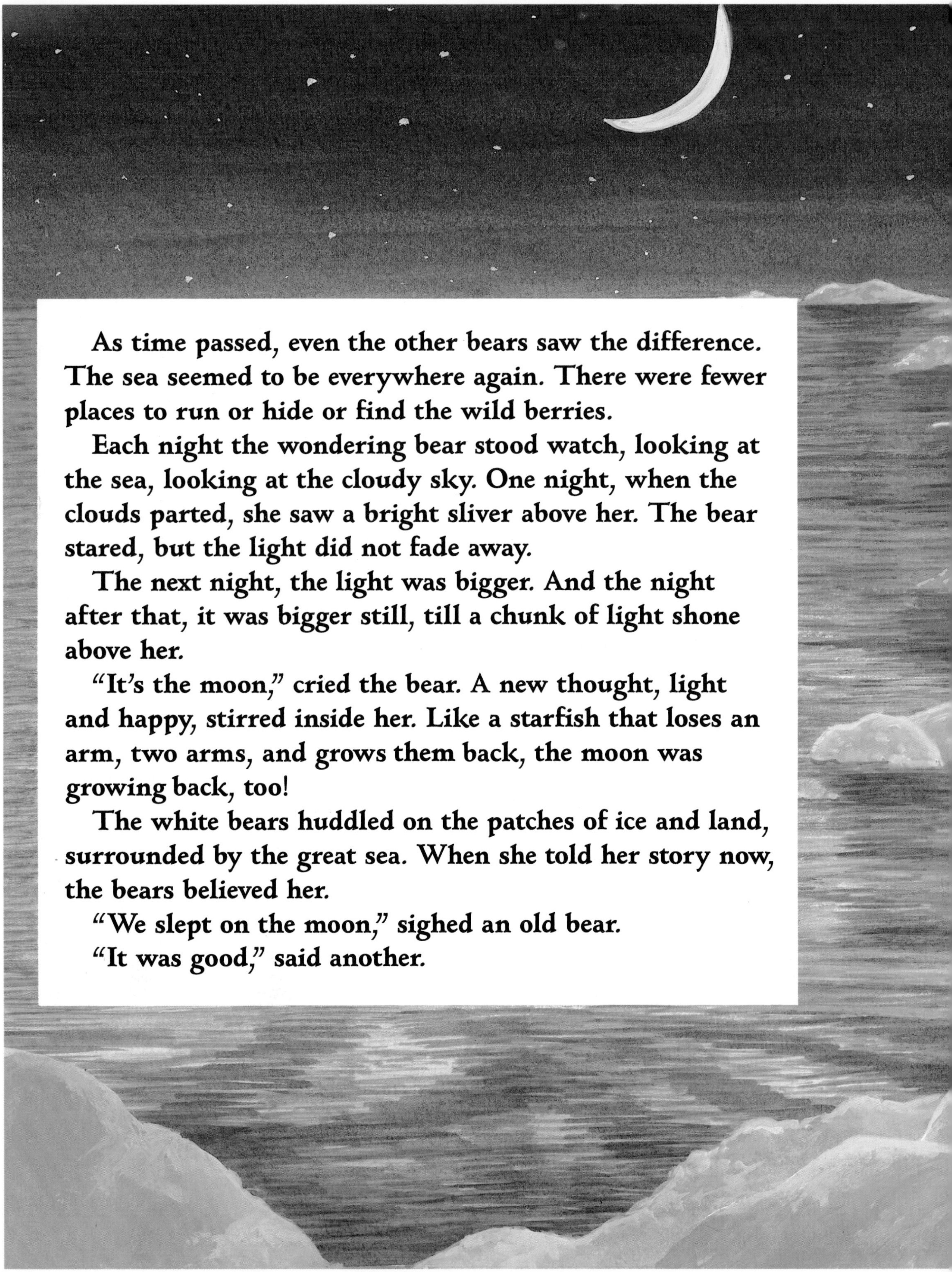

As time passed, even the other bears saw the difference. The sea seemed to be everywhere again. There were fewer places to run or hide or find the wild berries.

Each night the wondering bear stood watch, looking at the sea, looking at the cloudy sky. One night, when the clouds parted, she saw a bright sliver above her. The bear stared, but the light did not fade away.

The next night, the light was bigger. And the night after that, it was bigger still, till a chunk of light shone above her.

"It's the moon," cried the bear. A new thought, light and happy, stirred inside her. Like a starfish that loses an arm, two arms, and grows them back, the moon was growing back, too!

The white bears huddled on the patches of ice and land, surrounded by the great sea. When she told her story now, the bears believed her.

"We slept on the moon," sighed an old bear.

"It was good," said another.

Some bears left to climb the stair of lights to the moon. But none of them was strong enough to swim to the edge of the sea. Only one bear could do that.

So the brave young bear swam again to the edge of the sea and climbed up the shimmering, twisting lights.

And when she crept out on the moon, it was round and full, just as she first remembered it.

But far below, she saw the ice bears' world disappearing. The rocky land was sinking; the ragged ice was melting. Everywhere, bears were sliding into the sea.

The bear on the moon swung her powerful paw until a big chunk of moon sailed high—and fell down and down.

The bears swam to the ice bobbing in the sea and climbed up. One small bear ran ahead to stare at the full moon above her.

"Look," she said in a small, thin voice. "There's a bear up there. There's a bear on the moon. You can see her bright, white face."

All the white bears looked up then and saw her—a white bear on the bright moon.

That night was very long ago. But the great white bears say that, even today, the bear on the moon is watching them still.

Each month, she digs snow and ice and land and sends it down for bears to live on. Gradually, the moon disappears until there is just a sliver left in the sky. As the white bear leaves and climbs down the northern lights, the last sliver of moon slides down behind her. Then, for a few days the moon is gone, and the brave bear swims and hunts and rests with the other bears in their world. When the moon begins to grow again, she returns to the sky. You can see her then, ready to send more of the good ice and land the bears love.

At the top of the world, a winter night lasts a long time. It is then the old bears remember and tell their stories.

"This ice you're resting on was once the moon," they tell the big-eyed seals and the shy white foxes.

"Look up!" the old bears cry. "Look at the shining stars! They're just bits of icy moon that the white bear scattered and flung so high into the sky, they never came down."

And when the night is clear and the moon is full, mother bears tell their cubs of a bear who wondered about things, of the brave white bear who swam so far, and climbed so high, and ran on the moon.

Even today, the small white bears like to hear about her. And they stand on the ice, as high as they can, to look at the big white bear on the moon, watching over them, so very far away.

Watercolors were used for the full-color art.
The text type is 16 point Schneidler Black.

Inquiries should be addressed to
William Morrow and Company, Inc.,
1350 Avenue of the Americas
New York, N.Y. 10019

Printed in Hong Kong at South China Printing Company (1988) Ltd.

1 2 3 4 5 6 7 8 9 10

Library of Congress Cataloging-in-Publication Data

Ryder, Joanne.
The bear on the moon / Joanne Ryder ;
illustrations by Carol Lacey.
p. cm.
Summary: Relates how the great white bears that live at the top of
the world came to live on ice and snow.
ISBN 0-688-08109-6. –ISBN 0-688-08110-X (lib. bdg.)
[1. Polar bears–Fiction. 2. Moon–Fiction.]
I. Lacey, Carol, ill. II. Title.
PZ7.R9752Bg 1991
[E]–dc20 89-13133 CIP AC